Baptism 12-11-2012
To Connor
from Grandma Bonnie

And God saw it was good.

—Genesis 1:10

ZONDERKIDZ

The Berenstain Bears Discover God's Creation
Previously published by Reader's Digest Kids in 1994 as *The Berenstain Bears and the Big Picture*
Copyright © 1992, 2010 by Berenstains, Inc.
Illustrations © 1992, 2010 by Berenstains, Inc.

Requests for information should be addressed to:

Zonderkidz, *Grand Rapids, Michigan* 49530

Library of Congress Cataloging-in-Publication Data

Berenstain, Stan, 1923–2005
    The Berenstain Bears discover God's creation / created by Stan and Jan Berenstain ; with Mike Berenstain.
        p.   cm.
    Summary: When Mama Bear takes away the television remote control, Brother and Sister Bear discover the wonders that God has created all around them.
    ISBN 978-0-310-71936-6 (hardcover)
    [1. Stories in rhyme. 2. Nature—Fiction. 3. Play—Fiction. 4. Television—Fiction. 5. Bears—Fiction.] I. Berenstain, Jan, 1923- II. Berenstain, Michael. III. Title.
    PZ8.3.B4493Bhbd 2010
    [E]—dc22   2009037059

Editor: *Mary Hassinger*
Art direction: *Cindy Davis*

Printed in China

10 11 12 13 14 15 /LPC/ 28 27 26 25 24 23 22 21 20 19 18 17 16 15 14 13 12 11 10 9 8 7 6 5 4 3

The Berenstain Bears
Discover God's Creation

by Stan and Jan Berenstain
with Mike Berenstain

ZONDERVAN.com/
AUTHORTRACKER
follow your favorite authors

ZONDERkidz

Living
Lights™

Said Mama Bear,
"It seems to me,
you cubs watch
much too much TV!"

"Don't turn it off!
It isn't fair!"
"Don't turn it off!
Please, Mama Bear!"

"Watching all that
TV slush
will surely turn
your brains to mush.

"I will not argue.
You have no vote.
I will keep
the TV remote!"

"I beg you, Ma,
on bended knee.
Don't take away
our TV!"

But Ma was firm.
Ma knew her mind.
"No more TV
of any kind!

There's so much more
to do and see.
God gave you eyes
for more than TV!"

The cubs were stunned.
The cubs were shocked.

Those TV-watching bears
were rocked!

Then Brother had a bright idea.
"Look out the window, Sister Bear.
I see another
world out there."

It was Bear Country,
God's creation.
It was lovelier than
any old TV station.

They opened up
the door a crack.
Now there was
no turning back.

When those TV bears
stepped outside,
their TV eyes
opened wide.

There were such amazing
things to see.
The cubs forgot
that old TV.

There was stuff called grass,
things called trees,

and flying things
called birds and bees.
How did God
think up all these?

And way, way,
away up high,
a big blue thing
called the sky.

The cubs loved all
that God had done,
and knew they were in
for much more fun!

There were other cubs
to run and play with,

and when they got tired—
to sit and stay with.

There were playground things
to climb and slide on,

and other things
to climb and ride on.

There was a thing called weather.
Sometimes it rained.

One day it even
hurricaned!

But then that thing
called sun came out
and spread its warmth
and light about.

Said Brother Bear,
"Who needs TV?"
Said Sister Bear,
"TV? Not me!"

"God's creation,
we have found,
has a better picture
and better sound.

And worlds of wonder
all around!
Thanks, Lord,
for this world we've found!"

"That thing up there
called the moon
means that we should
go home soon!"

But when the cubs got home,
what did they see?
Their papa looking
at TV.

Maybe Papa didn't know
God's creation was better
than any old show!

"Papa! Too much of
that TV slush
will surely turn
your brain to mush!

Come outside,
and you will see
God's creation is much better
than any old TV!"